Dear Parents,

Welcome to the Scholastic Reader series. We have taken over 80 years of experience with teachers, parents, and children and put it into a program that is designed to match your child's interests and skills.

Level 1—Short sentences and stories made up of words kids can sound out using their phonics skills and words that are important to remember.

Level 2—Longer sentences and stories with words kids need to know and new "big" words that they will want to know.

Level 3—From sentences to paragraphs to longer stories, these books have large "chunks" of texts and are made up of a rich vocabulary.

Level 4—First chapter books with more words and fewer pictures.

It is important that children learn to read well enough to succeed in school and beyond. Here are ideas for reading this book with your child:

- Look at the book together. Encourage your child to read the title and make a prediction about the story.
- Read the book together. Encourage your child to sound out words when appropriate. When your child struggles, you can help by providing the word.
- Encourage your child to retell the story. This is a great way to check for comprehension.
- Have your child take the fluency test on the last page to check progress.

Scholastic Readers are designed to support your child's efforts to learn how to read at every age and every stage. Enjoy helping your child learn to read and love to read.

—**Francie Alexander**
Chief Education Officer
Scholastic Education

For Mom and Dad—
Thank you
–J.E.M.

For Edie Weinberg, who inspires
–B.L.

Text copyright © 2003 by Scholastic Inc.
Illustrations copyright © 2003 by Barbara Lanza.
All rights reserved. Published by Scholastic Inc.
SCHOLASTIC, CARTWHEEL BOOKS, and associated logos are
trademarks and/or registered trademarks of Scholastic Inc.

Library of Congress Cataloging-in-Publication Data
Mills, J. Elizabeth.
    Beauty and the beast / adapted by J. Elizabeth Mills; illustrated by Barbara Lanza.
       p.   cm. — (Scholastic readers. Level 2)
    Summary: Through her great capacity to love, a kind and beautiful maid releases a
handsome prince from the spell which has made him an ugly beast.
    ISBN 0-439-47151-6 (alk. paper)
    [1. Fairy tales.   2. Folklore — France.   I. Lanza, Barbara, ill.   II. Title.   III.
Series.
PZ8.M6345Be   2003
    398.2'0944'02—dc21
[E]
2002010772

12 11 10 9 8 7 6 5   06 07
Printed in the U.S.A. 23 • First printing, May 2003

Beauty
and the
Beast

Adapted by **J. Elizabeth Mills**

Illustrated by **Barbara Lanza**

Scholastic Reader — Level 2

SCHOLASTIC INC. Cartwheel ·B·O·O·K·S· ®

New York   Toronto   London   Auckland   Sydney
Mexico City   New Delhi   Hong Kong   Buenos Aires

A rich man had three daughters.

The older daughters were selfish and mean.

But the youngest daughter was sweet and kind.

Her name was Beauty.

The older sisters did not like Beauty.

The father owned many ships.

One day, his ships were lost at sea.

The family became poor.

The older sisters didn't like being poor.

They would not do any work.

Beauty didn't like being poor, either.
But she cleaned the house and cooked.

Then the father
heard that one ship was found.
"Hooray! We are rich again!"
said the oldest sister.
The father set off to meet his ship.
"What would you like me to bring back
to you?" he asked.

One daughter asked for dresses.

Another asked for jewels.

Beauty asked only for a rose.

But when he arrived,
the father saw the ship was ruined.
He had no money to buy dresses.
He had no money to buy jewels.

On his way home, the father passed a garden.
He picked a rose for Beauty.

Suddenly, he saw an ugly beast.

"That rose is mine!" said the Beast. "Now you must die!"

"The rose is for my daughter," said the father.

"Then she may come to my castle in your place," said the Beast. "But she must want to stay."

The father returned home.

He gave Beauty the rose and told his story.

"This is Beauty's fault," her sisters said.

"I will live with the Beast," said Beauty.

Her father tried to stop her.

But the next morning,

Beauty went to the castle.

"Do you want to stay here?"
the Beast asked.
"Yes," said Beauty.
"Will you marry me?" asked
the Beast.
"No," said Beauty.

For three months Beauty
stayed with the Beast.
He gave her beautiful dresses.
He gave her many books to read.
The Beast is very kind, thought Beauty.

Each evening Beauty and the Beast ate together.
Each evening he asked her to marry him.
And each evening she said "no."

One night, Beauty asked to see her family.

"You may go home," said the Beast. "But you must return in eight days."

Beauty promised to return.

Then the Beast asked her to marry him.

But again, Beauty said "no."

The next day, Beauty went home.

Her father was happy to see her.

But her sisters saw her beautiful clothes.

And they were jealous.

Eight days passed.

Beauty's sisters begged her not to leave.

So Beauty agreed to stay.

"Perhaps the Beast will be angry and eat her!"

they said to each other.

On the tenth night,
Beauty had a dream.
The Beast was dying.

Beauty awoke.

She felt scared and sad.

She had broken her promise.

Beauty rushed back to the Beast.

She found him in the garden.

"I'm sorry, Beast!" cried Beauty.

She kissed his ugly face.

"I know you have a good heart," she said.

"I will marry you."

Just then, there was a bright light.

A handsome prince stood before her.
"Where is the Beast?" she asked.

"I was the Beast," said the prince.
"But you saw my good heart
instead of my ugly face.
You broke the spell."

And Beauty and the prince
lived happily ever after.

Fluency Fun

The words in each list below end in the same sounds.
Read the words in a list.
Read them again.
Read them faster.
Try to read all 15 words in one minute.

light	**face**	**team**
night	**race**	**cream**
sight	**grace**	**dream**
bright	**place**	**steam**
flight	**space**	**scream**

Look for these words in the story.

daughter   **money**   **buy**

morning   **eight**

Note to Parents:

According to *A Dictionary of Reading and Related Terms,* fluency is "the ability to read smoothly, easily, and readily with freedom from word-recognition problems." Fluency is necessary for good comprehension and enjoyable reading. The activities on this page include a speed drill and a sight-recognition drill. Speed drills build fluency because they help students rapidly recognize common syllables and spelling patterns in words, and they're fun! Sight-recognition drills help students smoothly and accurately recognize words. Practice these activities with your child to help him or her become a fluent reader.

—**Wiley Blevins,**
Reading Specialist